Crow-
Magnum

Crow-Magnum

Laurel McHargue

STRACK PRESS

STRACK PRESS LLC | COLORADO

Crow-Magnum

Published by Strack Press LLC
Salida, CO

Copyright © 2020 by Laurel McHargue
All rights reserved by Laurel McHargue:
laurel@strackpress.com

FIRST EDITION 2020

ISBN: 978-1-945837-04-3

Cover Design by Laurel McHargue
Cover Art by Becky Jewell

PRINTED IN THE UNITED STATES OF AMERICA

Crow-Magnum

RUBY AND JADE sat in their pink 1959 El Dorado convertible at a T-intersection in the middle of nowhere for several moments, both staring right, and then left, and then right again before looking at one another. There was nothing familiar about the rolling hills to the right or the winding road to the left, and there was nothing to see through the thick trees to their front.

"Well, this is depressing." Ruby released her grasp on the steering wheel. The twins were lost, and the battery on their shared cell phone had died miles ago on their way home from a spelunking adventure.

"I've never seen a sky so gray. What do you think? Left or right?" Jade looked at their cell phone one last time before stashing it in the console. "I say we toss a coin. Anything to get away from this Texas Chainsaw Massacre vibe."

If they'd been city girls or scary movie fans, the whirr of a chainsaw in the distance might have frightened them.

"Don't worry, little sister, I know how to handle that .357." Ruby was grateful their father, John, had taught them how to wield even the most temperamental of power tools and how to handle the .357 Magnum revolver they carried in their glove compartment.

"Little sister!" Jade scoffed. "What am I, like, 30 seconds younger than you?"

"Hey, I clearly learned a lot in those 30 seconds! But look!" Ruby pointed to a crow flying high above them. It circled and disappeared.

"Weird, right?" Jade squinted into the dreary sky. The day was muggy and warm, and the open convertible top did little to cool the sweat from their bodies. "So, come on. You're the decisive one, *big* sister. Pick a direction!"

"I don't know. Neither one feels right. A GPS would've been handy. Not that there's any service out here. Can't believe we're still driving this old

Bazooka on wheels. We're so *not* pink-car girls." Ruby smacked the dashboard, and immediately felt guilty.

Their father had purchased the car two years earlier for their 18th birthday, shortly after their mother had died of "natural causes." Twenty now, the girls routinely laughed at their father's gaffe.

"Hey! Go easy on her, *Ellie May*!"

"Really, Jade? It's bad enough when those horny teenagers call me that!" Ruby flicked a mosquito off her arm.

"I know. Sorry. *Daisy Duke* and *Ellie May*. I don't get it. We don't even dress like those hillbillies."

"It's the identical twin thing. Every guy's fantasy, right? You know you've felt it since we were kids. And the car doesn't help. I know dad meant well, but if he knew the shit we keep getting from guys—"

"It'd break his heart. We'll never be able to trade it in for something more—"

"Appropriate? More *us*? Yeah, I know." Ruby smoothed her hand across the dash. As they often did, the girls seamlessly finished the other's thoughts.

Not every pair of twins shared a psychic connection, but Ruby and Jade did.

"Arrg!" Jade threw her head back and ruffled her raven-colored hair, scanning the flat gray sky. "That chainsaw's getting on my nerves."

"Wait! There it is again!" Ruby looked up at the crow, which greeted them with a cacophonous caw this time.

"She's been following us since we left the cave," said Jade. "Do you think it's the same one that was—"

"Hanging around Mom's window for days before she died?" Ruby never minced words. "I think so. And so do you." She scratched where the mosquito had bitten.

"Yeah. Something about the sound it makes." Jade giggled. "Sounds like Mom, scolding us for getting lost. '*You should have listened to your father and taken a paper map, just in case!*'"

Ruby laughed at her sister's impersonation. "She was about as old-fashioned as Dad, right? A paper map! But I really thought you had the backup charger for our phone."

"And I thought *you* had it. You think maybe we're old enough to have our own phones yet?"

"I dunno. It's not like you're ever that far from me." Ruby looked at her sister and smiled. She wouldn't admit it, but she felt more balanced when she was with Jade. More grounded.

"Oh, and now *you* sound just like Mom." Jade poked Ruby in the arm. "I'll give her credit, though. She sure could stretch a meal."

"And find a bargain. How she had the patience to sort through those thrift store racks, I'll never know." Ruby examined her clothes, smudged with dirt from the cave.

"She could sniff out the designers, too! Remember those Michael Kors jeans? They still had tags on them." Jade pouted. "Still bugs me they couldn't say why she died. It makes no sense, right? Do you ever even remember her being sick? You know, before she—"

"No." Ruby rubbed goosebumps from her brown arms and watched the crow circle overhead. She wasn't in any mood to discuss her mother's death. She often had to catch herself after grabbing the phone to text a message or share a photo, or even to call. She could still hear her mother's laughter.

Aiyana's death remained a mystery. None of the specialists could understand how she had gone from full vitality to a relentless decline over several months until her final day.

"And I'm worried about Dad. Doesn't seem like he wants to move on." Jade frowned.

"It's only been two years. Two years of us taking shit for driving this ridiculous car!" Ruby tried to lighten the mood, but to no avail.

The crow continued to circle overhead.

"Maybe you should kill the engine till our friend makes up her mind," Jade suggested. "I know we're going to end up following her. We can wait, but let's not run out of gas too."

"Good point." Ruby pulled over to the shoulder and killed the engine. "Hey, the cave was pretty cool, right? Be a great place to hide a body. They should make a Sherlock Holmes episode there."

"Wouldn't you just love to imagine your Benedict Cumber-crush filming nearby?" Jade taunted her sister.

"*You're* the one with a hard-on for him!" Ruby shoved her sister's arm, happy to be talking about anything other than their sorrow.

"Eeeww! That's just wrong! But yes. He's yummy. We'll share him. I wouldn't mind making *that* guy's fantasy come true!"

"Wow! You're bad," Ruby laughed, glancing at the undecided crow. "Let's play 'what if' while Rava makes up her mind."

"Rava?"

"Why not? Might as well give her a name if she's going to be hanging out with us."

"There's something odd about this crow. Do you feel it?" Jade asked. "It's not a bad feeling, but it's not exactly good, either."

"Yeah. It's just . . . different. Let's play." Ruby fidgeted in her seat.

"Okay. I'll start," said Jade. "What if we accidentally ate THC-laced brownies at a party?"

"Huh. Maybe we should try it sometime. Or maybe just you. I'll stay in control. Something tells me you'd be a hoot when you're high! Okay. What if we could fly just by thinking about it?" Ruby closed her eyes to imagine flying over the earth.

"That'd be awesome. We could be like Superman. No, Wonder Woman. We'll be protectors of the planet! You can keep the red bustier. Mine'll be green. We'll be Wonder Women! Okay. What if we were kidnapped and knew there was no way we'd ever escape or be rescued, even by our bootylicious Benedict?"

"Oh! Come on, now, you know he'd come to our rescue, especially when he finds out were twins! Here's a good one. What if Dad isn't our real father?" Ruby glanced at the still-circling crow.

"Well, I guess that would explain his choice in cars! But, if he isn't our father, then who could be? Let's not go there! My turn. What if we went blind?"

"Then we wouldn't have to drive this relic anymore! Ha!" Ruby smacked the steering wheel again and sighed. She saw Jade raise an eyebrow, waiting for her sister's next question. "Okay. Here's one, but you're not going to like it. What if . . . what if someone killed Mom?"

Jade's jaw dropped. "Not possible. She was a saint! Everyone said so! You're not asking that seriously, are you? That's horrible, Ruby. How could you?"

"I don't know. It's just that—"

"No. I can't even imagine. Just stop." Jade crossed her arms. "No more 'what ifs.' And OH—MY—GOD will that chainsaw ever stop?"

"I know, right? Feels like we're in a dentist office, doesn't it?" Ruby laughed joylessly. "I can almost smell burning tooth dust."

"Oh! Gross! Stop it! As if this isn't creepy enough." Jade shivered.

"I'd close the rooftop, but the breeze feels good."

"Whatever. I know you just want to watch Rava. And yeah, this is almost as bad as waiting for the drill. Remember Conroy's horrible hygienist, Clara?"

"*Clara, the Horrible Hygienist*! That'd make a great Stephen King children's book! How could I forget her?" Ruby chuckled. "The Marquis de Sade was probably her great-grandfather. And her breath! Holy shit!"

"No, just shit. Nothing holy about that snorting gum-gouger. Must've been embarrassing for Dad when he told Conroy we'd be switching dentists, but thank God Mom insisted."

"*There's a lesson for you girls,*" Ruby mimicked her father, "*never mix business with friendship.*"

"At least he kept bringing over free toothpaste samples!" Jade picked at something between her teeth.

"Yeah. We got all the fun flavors. And Mom always wanted '*only the least expensive brand, please.*' She was even frugal with free stuff! Dad never used what he gave us. And he probably still feels guilty over leaving Conroy's practice."

Both girls glanced at the crow.

"Why do you think Conroy and Ellen moved after Mom died?" Jade's voice was a whisper. "It's not like Conroy got a new job, and I heard their new place isn't much different."

"I don't know. Mom and Ellen were besties since we were little. Maybe it was too hard for her." Ruby frowned, angry at herself for having brought the conversation back to their mother.

"Too hard for *her*? What about Dad?" Jade crossed her arms again. "He was their friend too, and they abandoned him. They abandoned us. What kind of friend does that?"

"I don't know. Guess I'm just trying to come up with an excuse that makes sense." Ruby's brow furrowed as an old memory resurfaced. "Hey, remember those photos I showed you of Mom and Dad's anniversary a while ago?"

"The ones with Ellen looking like she had a fake smile? Didn't we decide she was probably having one of her infamous gas attacks from visiting the cheese platter too many times?"

Ruby laughed. "Yeah, those. Remember I also said I thought the way Conroy was looking at Mom seemed a bit . . . I don't know . . . more than just friendly?"

"And I told you to stop being such an amateur sleuth. Don't go there, Ruby. That's just gross. He was our science tutor, for God's sake, and Ellen edited our English papers. They're practically . . . they *were* practically our aunt and uncle." Jade scrunched her lips together.

The crow startled them from their funk with another loud caw before descending toward them in a gentle spiral. They watched in awe as it landed on the hood of their El Dorado. Its shiny blackness contrasted stunningly against the pink paint, and its sharp claws clip-clopped tentatively as it marched in a circle. The crow released another cry into the flat gray sky. Soon, another crow answered and joined the first. Ruby and Jade looked from the birds to one another and back to the birds again, their eyebrows raised in disbelief.

"Looks like Rava was just waiting for her friend," said Ruby.

The two birds hopped to the top edge of the windshield and stared into the twins' eyes.

Mesmerized, they stared back, and time seemed to stand still.

"Ahhh, are you feeling what I'm feeling?" Jade asked.

"Yeah, and are you seeing what I'm seeing? Are their eyes glowing?"

"Yup. And growing?"

"Uh-huh!" Ruby leaned forward, her eyes locked on those of the bird in front of her. "It feels like I'm falling into her eyes. Did we eat something wacky back at the cave?"

"No, I don't think so." Jade stared into the new crow's eyes. "Should we let them do what I think they're asking?"

"Well, if you want me to make this decision too, I'll say yes. This is just so . . . weird and exciting, right?"

"Yup. I'm not afraid. Go for it, Shadow."

"Did she just tell you her name?" Ruby asked, still mesmerized by her crow.

"Yup. I heard it, or felt it, or something."

A moment later, the girls felt a tickling flutter of feathers on their cheeks as the birds lit atop their heads.

"Ahh . . .," Ruby looked at her sister, "their claws kinda feels like those wiry head massager thingies sold '*Only on TV*,' am I right?"

"Uh-huh. Wait a minute. They stopped moving."

"Whoa!" Ruby's eyes grew wide. "Who's that? Are you seeing this? It's like I'm looking through a fuzzy tunnel! What the—"

"If you're seeing a dude in a baseball cap, then yeah. He's locking the outside door of some office building. I can't see his face, though, can you? And . . . Ruby . . . what the fuck?"

"I don't know! He's putting a gym bag into his trunk. Go ahead and call me an amateur sleuth, but the dude looks like he's sneaking around. Like he's hiding something."

"No, I agree. He's driving off now."

The crows disengaged abruptly and hopped back onto the top edge of the windshield.

"What just happened?" Both girls asked simultaneously before looking back at the crows.

"Not sure," said Ruby, "but . . . and don't ask me how or why, but I think they're trying to tell us something."

The crows gazed into the girls' eyes one more time before taking flight and soaring side by side down the hill to their left. Ruby knew this was her cue to follow. She finally had a direction to turn, even if the decision had been made by crows.

"Good riddance, chainsaw." Ruby started the engine, pulled onto the road, and turned left. A brilliant beam of setting sunlight broke through the overcast ahead of them, briefly illuminating the birds. "I'll take that as a good sign. Let's see where they'll take us, shall we, Watson?"

"Oh, so I'm the sidekick?" Jade asked.

"But of course! If you recall, you're the one who volunteered to wear the *green* bustier!"

"Yeah, okay, guilty as charged." Jade chuckled, and then murmured, "Doc's more sensible anyway."

The girls were quiet for a while as they followed the crows, which were never out of sight.

"Look! I recognize that road," Ruby said, turning on her blinker. "I know the way home from here." She relaxed her shoulders.

But the birds remained on a straight path beyond the turnoff.

"I know you're ready to go home, but—"

"But they're taking us somewhere else, right?" Ruby finished Jade's thought. "Are you up for it, or are we just being stupid?" She would trust Jade's judgement.

"Let's keep following. At least until we have to refuel. If we have to stop and they keep flying away, then maybe we're just being silly because we're overtired. Deal?"

"Deal. They're trying to show us something. I have no idea how or why, but I just know it, and I know you feel it too."

Jade nodded, her eyes locked onto the mysterious crows.

Ruby wouldn't say it, but she believed the crows' appearance had something to do with their mother.

Several miles beyond the turnoff Ruby had hoped to take, the crows flew toward the next town beyond their own. It was the town where Ellen and Conroy had moved, though they'd never invited their old friends to visit. Twenty minutes later, the crows slowed and circled over the top of a house at the end of a long, sparsely populated road.

"Isn't that the car we saw in our vision?" Jade whispered, though there was no one around to hear her but her sister.

"Yeah. Hey, it's getting dark, but these wheels'll stand out like a six-foot tall redhead in China. Let's park farther down the street and see what's up."

The birds seemed to approve of their decision. They landed on the hood of the car again and hopped to the top of the windshield. When they locked eyes with the girls as they had before, Ruby and Jade knew what was coming next: a flutter of feathers and a perch upon their heads. This time, the visions they relayed were horrifying.

"Oh, shit!" Ruby whispered.

Like Odin's ravens Huginn and Muninn, the crows relayed the thoughts and memories of the man in the house to the twins. But instead of by whispers, they communicated via their claws, spread through the girls' thick black hair and strategically anchored onto specific spots.

"It's Conroy. He looks pissed," said Jade.

Their old neighbor was alone, and pouring himself a generous double of Jameson. He picked up a photo of his wife from his fireplace mantle and smashed it into the open fireplace.

"You think you can just leave me?" he screamed at the cold bricks. "You're just like all of them. You just wait. I'll find a way to get you like I got Aiyana."

The girls both gasped and grabbed hands, startling the crows from the perch on their heads and back onto the windshield where they waited for the girls to settle down. They waited for many minutes while Ruby and Jade stared at one another before bursting into hushed discussion about the brief vision.

"What the fuck, Jade! I told you something wasn't right about him!"

"But . . . but . . . Conroy? What did he do? Ellen left him? I don't understand!" There were tears in Jade's eyes.

Without answering her sister, Ruby turned back to the birds. "Show us more," she demanded, "and Jade, you need to stay calm, understand?"

Jade nodded and wiped her eyes, and the birds returned atop the girls' heads, Rava on Ruby's, Shadow on Jade's.

The next vision was from Conroy's memory, and the girls could see their mother through the man's eyes—his longing, fantasizing eyes. They could hear his internal dialogue.

"Why did she pick him? What could I have done to make her realize she should be with me— that she should leave that lowlife scum that got her pregnant? What's wrong with me, or is she like all the others—thinking she's too good for me? Me, a successful doctor! But she stays with that sweaty ranch hand instead. Makes no sense. Didn't she notice my glances? Didn't she feel the electricity whenever I touched her? Didn't I show up whenever she needed a favor? Well, if I can't have her—"

"Oh my God," Ruby whispered, "he's deranged."

They watched as Conroy formulated his plan years ago when he finally accepted Aiyana would not leave her husband and run away with him. It was a simple, brilliant plan. All he had to do was add a little something to the tube of cheap toothpaste he routinely delivered with a smile along with the others. Aiyana was the only one in the household who used that formula, so there'd be no chance of harming the girls.

Conroy's inner thoughts continued. *"Hurting the twins would be wrong. They're still too young to break a man's heart."*

"The toothpaste," Jade whispered, her eyelids fluttering in the vision as it continued.

Once Conroy had the toothpaste tube crimper, the rest was easy. He'd start by adding just a bit of his concoction to the paste, and once Aiyana started exhibiting signs of illness, he'd increase the amount slowly with each new tube. No one would think to test for his newly fabricated chemical, and she'd eventually succumb to the poison.

The girls were suddenly in Conroy's head at their mother's funeral.

"Good job, ol' boy! Brilliant as always! Too bad that bitch wasn't smart enough to see how much better her life would have been with me."

And then the man's thoughts jumped to the present.

"We have to stop him!" Jade whispered. "He's planning to find Ellen and—"

"Kill her," Ruby finished. "He thinks she's going to go to the police. He's going to kill her and leave the country. He's going to keep killing, Jade. He's sick."

Still experiencing visions from the crows, the girls watched Conroy pace back and forth in front of his fireplace, babbling to himself.

"Yeah, a nice long vacation," he said. "Plenty of other stupid women in relationships with mediocre men. I'll relieve them of their burdensome lives." He kicked a wooden stool. "I'll take my time. No one'll ever find out."

But the crows knew what he'd done. And so, now, did the girls. What the birds planted in their minds was startling. It was also thrilling. A new kind of justice was being offered.

"We need to make a decision, Jade."

"You make it," Jade whispered. "I'll do whatever you decide."

"No. We make this one together. Yes or no, on the count of three. One . . . two . . ."

On the count of three, both girls whispered "Yes."

There was no time to question why the crows had waited more than two years to show them the truth—Conroy was readying himself to leave his house. Perhaps the birds knew the girls had needed time to mature and harden their emotions. Perhaps they wanted to ensure the girls were up for the responsibilities ahead, the ones that would follow this grim task.

It didn't matter. Rava and Shadow made it clear that the girls were at a turning point in their lives.

The crows disengaged and flew to the hood of the car.

"We could still drive away, right now," Ruby offered. "We could raise this wonky roof and drive away, go get a pizza and pretend this never happened. We could go home, recharge this stupid phone, and help Dad set up a dating profile."

"Or we can do what Shadow and Rava are suggesting. Do we really have a choice, Ruby? Can you let Mom's murderer walk free, knowing he's already planning to kill again?"

"We could call the police—"

"And say what? Even if we could call them, which we can't, there's no way they'll believe our story. They'll want answers. They'll want to know how we knew about Conroy. And what'll we say? 'Oh, well, you see, officers, these two crows told us everything.' They'll lock *us* up!"

"Okay, okay. But we wait till he comes outside, right? And then . . . and then . . ."

Jade opened the glove compartment, checked the cylinder of the .357 to ensure it was loaded, and handed the gun to her sister. "You have the steadier hand," she said, as if they'd practiced this drill countless times before.

The crows watched from the top of the windshield.

Both girls got out of the car and took slow steps toward the house. Ruby let the handgun hang by her side. Beads of sweat gathered on her foreheads and under her arms.

"We've only practiced at the range, Jade. What if I can't do it?"

"Conroy poisoned Mom."

"Right. Right. Shit! He's opening his door! Stay near me, Jade."

"I'm right here. We can do this."

The girls stopped at the end of Conroy's driveway and waited for him to see them. When he did, he jumped back, nearly tumbled over a shrub, and let out a high-pitched exclamation. He squinted in the darkness toward them, and when it was clear he recognized them, he opened his arms to them.

"Girls! What a lovely surprise! I've been meaning to invite you over, but—"

He dropped his arms when Ruby raised hers.

"We know what you did, you sonovabitch," Jade said.

"Why? Why'd you do it? We were your friends! We treated you like family!" Ruby kept the weapon pointed at that man, whose hands were now held out in front of him, as if they could stop a bullet.

"Oh, now, surely you couldn't pull the trigger on an old friend, girls! You're not murderers! Look! I'll go to the police first thing in the morning and turn myself in, I swear. There's just something very important I need to do tonight. Put down the gun, now. I'm an important man, you know. I'll do the right thing. You do the right thing too."

For a moment, Ruby waivered. He had a point. She wasn't a murderer. And could she truly pull the trigger on an old friend? But just as she was lowering her weapon, Rava settled back onto her head and showed her the thoughts streaming through Conroy's mind in real time. He was laughing inside. He knew neither of the twins could harm him.

"You're stupid, scared girls," he was thinking. *"I can see it on your faces and in the dark sweat stains on your shirts. I'll send you home believing my promise, I'll carry out my plan for Ellen, and be on the next flight to the Netherlands. You're just stupid girls, as stupid as your mother was."*

Ruby raised her weapon again; it would be an easy shot to the heart at less than 20 feet. Could she kill him? Of course she could. This was not some kindly old neighbor. This was a deceptive, evil man who'd planned and executed a brilliant murder without regard for the other lives he'd destroyed or remorse for what he'd done.

Conroy appeared ready to bolt, and as Ruby moved her finger onto the trigger, the crow stopped her with a vision and an offer. Yes, she could pull the trigger—she had made the decision, was ready to, and wanted to. But the crow's plan was stunning.

"Jade, send Shadow, now!"

Jade looked at her crow and, in an unwavering voice, said, "Fire when ready." Instantly, Shadow flew toward Conroy, threatening him from above with a raucous *caw* that sounded more to the girls like *kill*.

"What the hell?" Conroy yelled, raising his arms to bat the bird away, and Rava disengaged from Ruby's head.

As Conroy struggled to fend off Shadow, the girls watched as Rava flew high into the darkening sky until she nearly disappeared before returning like a missile. Just before impacting the place Ruby's bullet would have pierced, Rava's black beak lengthened into a razor-sharp point and her feathers transformed into segmented, articulating armor, spreading down to protect her body just before impact.

The expression on Conroy's face before he hit the ground was one the girls would never forget—it was an expression of disgust, contempt, and utter disbelief.

The following morning, Conroy's mail deliverer called the police after seeing the man on the ground. He was at a loss for how to describe the man's wound.

"It looks like there's, ah, a really big hole through his heart from front to back," he said, his voice trembling.

When the police and coroner arrived, they too were confused.

"Look here," the coroner pointed. "Crow tail feathers on the ground. And there's one stuck to this shattered rib. Odd."

"Been a lot of crows in town this year," said a police officer, as if that explained anything.

"Over here!" another officer called from the back of Conroy's vehicle. He pulled out several vials of mysterious liquid and an abundance of travel-size toothpaste tubes from a gym bag in Conroy's trunk. "Better get these to the lab."

The twins woke to a hubbub in their front yard. Reporters had gotten wind of a story connecting the dead dentist to John's family.

"We tell him nothing, Jade. Just that the cave was awesome and we stayed longer than we'd planned."

Jade nodded. "Ah, Dad?" she knocked on her father's bedroom door. "We heard something on the radio this morning. You might want to come out here."

"Something about Conroy," Ruby added, talking loudly through the door. "The police want to talk with anyone who's been his patient, and there are reporters outside. We're heading out now. You might want to put on pants."

They went to the back door, and as they opened it, a realization hit them at the same time, as it often had in the past. Ruby spoke first.

"He's not the last vicious criminal out there, you know."

"We should stay in school, though. We'll need a cover."

"We're really doing this, then? You're with me? Because I don't think I can to this without you, little sister."

Jade nodded.

"This is no game, Jade. This means we're hunters now—and not for meals."

"I know." Jade faced Ruby and took her sister's hands into her own.

A sudden ruckus from the reporters startled them. Their father had opened the front door.

"And we can't tell anyone." Ruby's voice was hushed, but intense. "Our lives won't be easy. And it won't be like your Wonder Women fantasy—we don't have superpowers."

"No, but for whatever reason, we do have something special on our side."

"We'll be taking justice into our own hands. We could get caught. They could lock us up, and then what would happen to Dad?"

"We won't let that happen, Ruby. Rava and Shadow won't let that happen. You felt it last night, didn't you? That we'd be safe? That we were meant to be there?"

Ruby nodded. She had felt it. She gave her sister a bear hug and the two snuck out the back door.

Avoiding the crowd at the front of their house, they made their way to the pink El Dorado and buckled up.

"I wonder when we'll get our next mission," said Ruby. "Seems we made it to Conroy's place just in time."

"We avenged Mom's murder last night, Ruby. Damn. It's just hitting me now." Jade squeezed her eyes closed, but not before tears fell.

Ruby wondered why she hadn't been able to cry yet. She looked up to see Rava soaring in a slow circle overhead before landing on the hood of the car. Shadow followed closely behind.

"Where to next, girls?" Ruby asked. No time for tears today.

Rava squawked, and then she and Shadow flew north.

Jade wiped her eyes, tied her hair back into a neat ponytail, and said, "Let's do this."

"Yeah. Let's. And what do you say we name this ol' car?"

"I'd say that's the best idea you've had today!"

With a full charge on their cell phone and a paper map under their seat, the twins drove north toward their next unknown encounter. They'd made a decision to dole out a new kind of justice in a world controlled by those who thought they were too clever to get caught after committing heinous crimes against innocents.

Their adventures had just begun.

Two Crows Artwork by Becky Jewell

NOTE:

The first edition of this story was published in **DARK EBB: Grim Tales (Volume 1)**, a collection of 19 bizarre short stories by Laurel McHargue, on April 1, 2020.

If you would like to read about more crime-solving adventures with Ruby, Jade, and their new crow companions, please let Laurel know . . . and post a review on Amazon!

ABOUT THE AUTHOR

Laurel McHargue, a 1983 graduate of West Point, is the author of books in multiple genres, including the award-winning fantasy trilogy *Waterwight*, and the host of the podcast
Alligator Preserves.
A former Army Officer and public school teacher, she now lives and laughs and publishes and podcasts in Colorado's Rocky Mountains, where she also raises ducks.

Read more of her short stories in her award-winning collection
DARK EBB: Grim Tales (Volume 1).

A Few More Words from Laurel

I would love to hear from you! Connect with me here:

Facebook: Leadville Laurel (author page)
Twitter: @LeadvilleLaurel
LinkedIn: Laurel (Bernier) McHargue
Web Page: www.laurelmchargue.com
Email: laurel@strackpress.com
Podcast: Alligator Preserves

Check out my other books on my **Amazon Author page**
and let me know what you think!

And remember, we struggling authors/musicians/artists/actors love positive feedback, so if you like what we do, please consider writing reviews of our work! If you don't like what we do, well, if you can't say something nice . . .

;)

Also by Laurel McHargue:

Waterwight: Book I of the Waterwight Series: In a post-cataclysmic world threatened by stinking ooze, a brave girl searches for her missing parents with the help of talking animals and evolving powers…while a malicious shapeshifter tries to stop her!

Waterwight Flux: Book II: Has Celeste cured the chaos in her shattered world? Nick and the villagers must defend themselves without her, and jealous ancient gods have selfish ideas about how they'll use the girl who stopped the ooze!

Waterwight Breathe: Book III: Celeste regains consciousness with powerful new abilities. The gods are in trouble, and Celeste must decide how, or if, she will help them. With insane scientists plotting to subjugate her village, she and her friends rally for a final confrontation!

DARK EBB: Grim Tales: A mysterious gift, tap shoes in a halfway house, alien orbs . . . and what's in the basement? Laurel McHargue's debut collection of short stories ranges in mood from somber to surreal with splashes of dark humor. CIPA EVVY Award Finalist!

The Hare, Raising Truth: Aeron doesn't know how good he has it. When he discovers the magic powers in a crusty old rabbit's foot, he believes the good luck charm will deliver him from his unlucky past. But will he *really* get lucky with the new girl?

Hunt for Red Meat (love stories): Photos, quotes, hunting tips and haiku poems enhance this humorous exploration of hunting, and Laurel demonstrates how hunting with one's partner can engender feelings of love in the wild!

Haikus Can Amuse!: Perfect homeschooling tool! Discover the creativity this haiku book will unleash in you! Explore your emotional responses as you complete unique poems with 366 first-line prompts and topics provided for you.

"Miss?": Maggie, a feisty young Army veteran, believes her new life as a 7th grade English teacher will be a breeze, but quickly finds out how wrong she is. Despite daily challenges, however, she finds ways to reach her struggling students, and must ultimately make a painful decision.

Hai CLASS ku: A fun homeschooling tool! A full semester's worth of daily Language Arts activities! Discover the creativity this haiku book will unleash in students! Ninety first-line prompts and topics provided to stimulate the imagination, with space to draw and journal.